Jungle Buddies

BY
DEBORAH GRADY

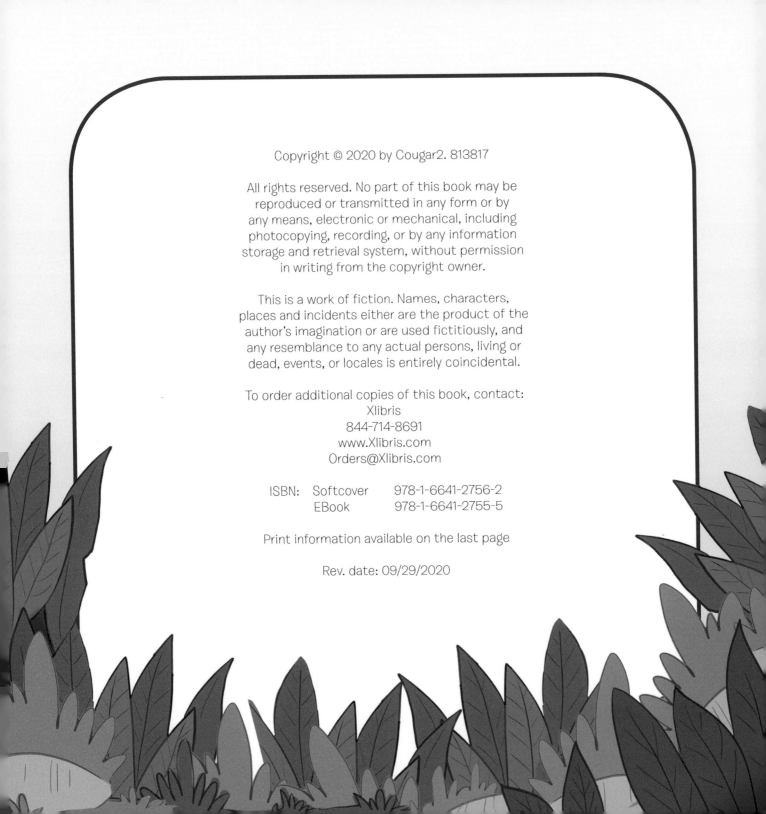

To order additional copies of this book, contact:
Xlibris
844-714-8691
www.Xlibris.com
Orders@Xlibris.com

ISBN: Softcover   978-1-6641-2756-2
        EBook   978-1-6641-2755-5

Print information available on the last page

Rev. date: 09/29/2020

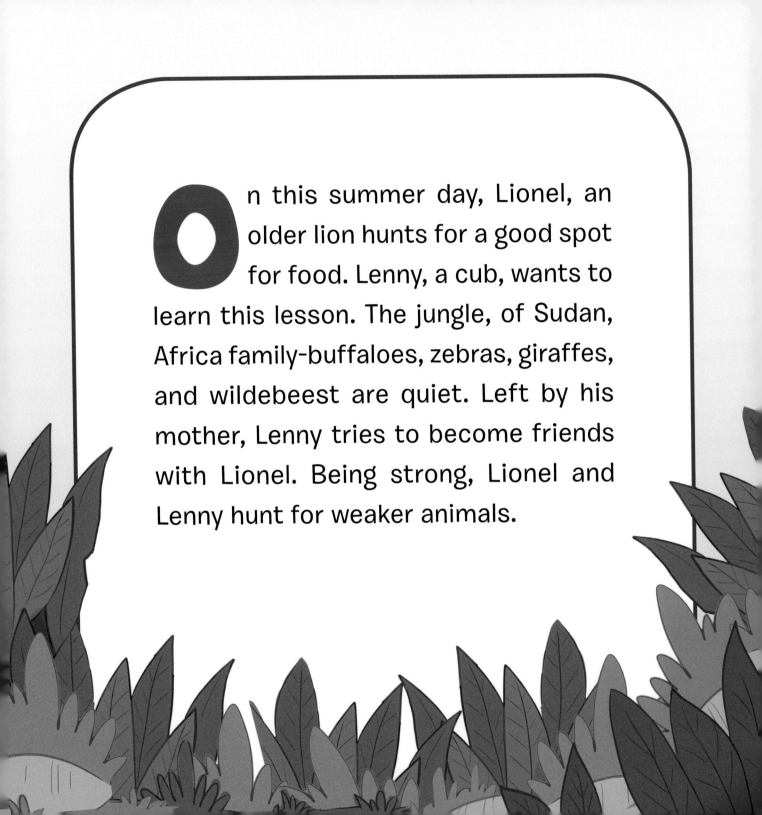

On this summer day, Lionel, an older lion hunts for a good spot for food. Lenny, a cub, wants to learn this lesson. The jungle, of Sudan, Africa family-buffaloes, zebras, giraffes, and wildebeest are quiet. Left by his mother, Lenny tries to become friends with Lionel. Being strong, Lionel and Lenny hunt for weaker animals.

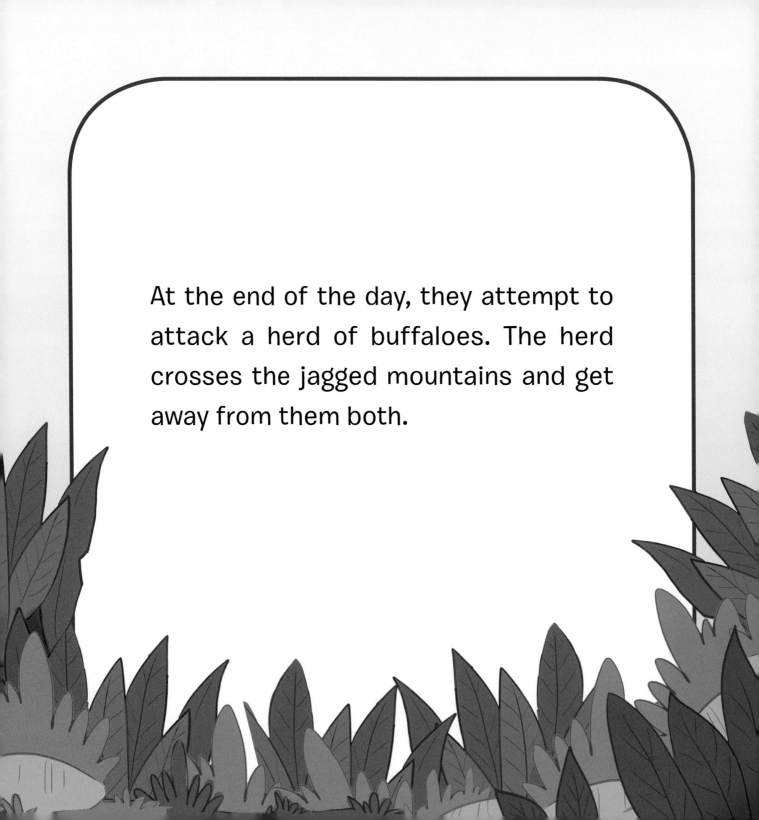

At the end of the day, they attempt to attack a herd of buffaloes. The herd crosses the jagged mountains and get away from them both.

Living is the lesson to learn. Lenny and Lionel rest on several boulders deciding on what to eat this day. The sun is very hot, Lionel wants Lenny to climb the nearby tree with him so they may rest.

Lionel climbs the high tree on the cliff first.

"Now, it's your turn!" Lionel yells.

"So here I come," says Lenny.

"Please try not to fall!" shouts Lionel.

Lenny inches next to Lionel but as soon as Lionel yells, Lenny suddenly slips and down he comes. Lenny tries to climb up again. This time, although shaky, he has success. Up in the tree, the two look down over a herd of wildebeest.

Both think one would be a tasty meal.

The wildebeest sense their presence and scatter from the brush.

Instead of eating, they grow tired and fall asleep without a kill.

The morning comes quickly; their stomachs empty. They wander along and find a herd of giraffes. Just as before, they are not quick enough. The chase finds them quite tired.

After this try, they know they need to stick together.

Lionel and Lenny hope they find food within a week.

The jungle is too much for Lenny.

Both stop and drink from the nearby watering hole, thinking of what their afternoon meal would be.

Life will be better in time. Lenny and Lionel knew the jungle will bring work as well as death.

Lionel likes Lenny and they become best friends. Everyday there will be new challenges and will be hard surviving!

So ends their adventure for now; as the sun begins to set.